Books by the same author

Solomon Smee Versus the Monkeys

Maisie Morris and the Whopping Lies

Jake Jellicoe and the Dread Pirate Redbeard

Candy Plastic

Maisie Morris and the Awful Arkwrights

Joanna Nadin

illustrated by Arthur Robins

WALKER BOOKS
AND SUBSIDIARIES

LONDON • BOSTON • SYDNEY • AUCKLAND

First published 2003 by Walker Books Ltd
87 Vauxhall Walk, London SE11 5HJ

4 6 8 10 9 7 5 3

Text © 2003 Joanna Nadin
Illustrations © 2003 Arthur Robins

The right of Joanna Nadin and Arthur Robins to be identified as author and illustrator respectively of this work has been asserted by them in accordance with the Copyright, Designs and Patents Act 1988

This book has been typeset in Randumhouse and Shinn Light

Printed in China

British Library Cataloguing in Publication Data:
a catalogue record for this book
is available from the British Library

ISBN 978-0-7445-9091-3

www.walkerbooks.co.uk

To my grandparents –
especially Grandpa Gaston

Contents

Getting old

Odd things happen when you grow up. Hair starts sprouting where there was no hair before. You get smellier and sulkier, wear strange clothes, and spend too much time indoors watching television. The good thing is that it doesn't last long, and after a few years you emerge from your dark and sweaty bedroom as a fully fledged grown-up.

But a word of warning: if you think growing up is bad, just wait. This is just a practice run. Because once you've become a grown-up, something even more whopping will happen. Something that will really make your stomach squirm.

The hair on top of your head will fade and turn grey or even fall out altogether, and new tufts will come out of your ears and nostrils instead. You will start to smell slightly fusty as well. Why, my very own grandpa has a distinct odour of cabbage and cod liver oil, and his lugholes are hairier than a marmoset's bottom! And all because he has grown old. And the older grannies and grandpas get, the more they need looking after, which is why we have old people's homes. These are big grand houses with lots of pastel-coloured bedrooms where old people can watch telly and play games all day. They don't have to wash up or cook or even wipe their own bottoms.

Gosh! What a fantastic place, you may think. It sounds a good deal better than 14 Lancelot Street, where I have to wash up the dinner plates, tidy my room and wipe my own bottom. Perhaps I'll move in with my grandpa, who is clearly being spoiled rotten.

A splendid idea – all children should spend as much time with their grandparents as possible. But some grandmas and grandpas don't have such a super time. In fact, a few have a downright rotten beastly time. This is because they live in the bottom right-hand corner of England in a very small and very dull town called Groutley.

Withering Heights

On the outskirts of Groutley, home of the not-so-famous Hosepipe Museum, and Peabody and Nidgett's department store, which only stocked extra-large tweed suits and doilies, sat a large grey creaky-looking building. It had a small spindly turret on one side, an overgrown garden and a pair of enormous iron gates on which was nailed a hand-painted sign that was starting to peel.

WITHERING HEIGHTS
RETIREMENT HOME
TAKING CARE OF YOUR AGEING
RELATIVES SO YOU DON'T HAVE TO
Proprietors
MR & MRS TREVOR ARKWRIGHT
GROUTLEY 522319

Now, I expect you think that doesn't sound too bad at all – a lick of paint and a quick mow of the lawn and Bob's your uncle, a home fit for the Queen of Sheba, let alone Granny Fletcher.

Well, firstly, Bob is not my uncle, as I repeatedly have to tell strangers who seem to think that they are acquainted with my family tree, when clearly they have never met me or my five sisters, three brothers and whippet before. Charlie is my uncle and he sells radiator valves in Chipping Sodbury.

Secondly, it wasn't the house or garden that was the problem, although the plumbing was temperamental and, you're right, it could have done with a new coat of paint. The problem was those last words on the bottom of the peeling sign on the gate. *Proprietors Mr & Mrs Trevor Arkwright.*

They were not actually both called Trevor; it is just that when grown-ups get married they like to write their names in this way because they think it's clever. It isn't. Anyway, that is not the point. The point is that the sort of people you want proprietoring such an establishment are the smiley, jolly-faced kind who can fix broken pipes and cook squidgy chocolate cake, and who never cheat at Monopoly.

Unfortunately Mr and Mrs Arkwright were none of the above.

12

Mrs Cynthia Arkwright (see, I told you she wasn't called Trevor) was a tall, bony, poisonous pest of a woman with an enormous dyed hairdo that looked like a fox, and too much fuchsia-coloured lipstick. She hated cooking, cleaning and plumbing, and *always* cheated at Monopoly. But, worst of all, she hated old people. She hated the way they always ate pilchards; she hated the way they wore overcoats in summer; and most of all she hated the way everyone else in the world seemed convinced they were somehow magical and wise.

"I don't know what all the fuss is about, Trevor," she would say to Mr Arkwright at breakfast. "What's wise about dribbling and playing whist all day? Clever? Ha! There's nothing clever about saggy bottoms and wrinkles. Yeeuch!" And she would readjust the Sellotape she used to keep her own wrinkles stretched tight at night and which made her look as though she were stuck permanently on the down bit of a roller coaster. "The sooner someone invents a never-get-old pill the better!"

13

"That's right, my petal," Mr Arkwright would say, his gold tooth gleaming as brightly as his oily hair and crocodile-skin shoes. "And I will buy you the very first pill that rolls off the production line."

Mr Arkwright would have hated old people too if he ever noticed them, but he was far too busy studying horse racing and thinking about scrap metal. He was a nasty, slippery sort of man who wore too much brown double-stitched nylon. He had made an awful lot of money selling second-hand cars, largely because his silver tongue and gold tooth managed to convince customers that the rusty banger in front of them, held together with cow gum and string, was in fact a tip-top quality bargain. And all the money he made he spent on buying more operations to make Mrs Arkwright look younger. "I'm all self-made and she's all man-made," he was fond of saying too loudly at parties. Which was true. So far Mrs Arkwright had had her bosom enlarged, her nose shrunk, her lips plumped, her legs stretched and her knees deknobbled. Like one of Mr Arkwright's clapped-out cars she had been pulled apart and stuck together again so many times, it was a wonder her innards didn't flop out onto her cornflakes.

All in all they were a revolting couple of con artists who only ran Withering Heights because they liked money and discovered that the more old people they charged to live in their house, and the less they looked after them, the more they could spend on themselves.

You may be wondering why on earth anyone would send their poor granny to live with such horrors, which is a very good question. And here's the answer.

When families arrived at Withering Heights with their unwanted relations, Mr and Mrs Arkwright would turn themselves into the very models of charm.

"My, what a lovely moustache your mother has, Mrs Fletcher," Mrs Arkwright would say. "Oh, and look at her wonderful warty fingers!"

"Of *course* we'll take care of her poodle as well," Mr Arkwright would add.

And – of course – poor Mrs Fletcher would hand

over her mother, together with an enormous cheque, before driving swiftly back the way she came, happy in the thought that she could get back to sherry evenings with Granny in such a safe pair of hands.

But the moment those enormous wrought-iron gates clanked shut, Mr and Mrs Arkwright would confiscate the poodle, pay the cheque into their own bank account and send Granny to bed without any supper. Never mind if she had once been the south of England tiddlywinks champion, or single-handedly stopped the Belgians invading Whitby.

No, to Mr and Mrs Arkwright, old people meant one thing and one thing only – money.

"They don't need it anyway," Mrs Arkwright declared as she spent another poor granny's savings on evening gowns and chocolates. "They'll only waste it on hairnets and cats."

What this needed, of course, was the man from the council to come round with his clipboard and disapproving tone and shut the whole house down. But, unfortunately, the man from the council, who incidentally was called Reg Yonkers, was far too busy dealing with a nasty spate of dog droppings which had spread from the municipal roses outside the not-so-famous Hosepipe Museum, past the Bernard Gibbons Memorial Multi-Storey Car Park and all the way down to the Razzmatazz Roller Rink.

If this were a normal tale of superheroic stunts and bravado, there would have been someone with a heart of gold and nerves of steel hidden away in Withering Heights, ready to call the man from the council and tell him to ditch the dog droppings and arrest Mr and Mrs Arkwright at once!

Well, there *was* someone hidden away, actually. Right up in the spindly turret lived the housekeeper,

Mrs Marigold Morris, and her small daughter, Maisie. They might not have had supernova stun guns or even an eagle-eyed action figure to thwart the evil Mrs Arkwright. In fact, right now they were far too busy to be thinking about amazing deeds of daring, because not only had Mrs Morris got beds to change, kippers to broil and at least seventeen bottoms to polish, but she also had to take up Maisie's brand-new second-hand school uniform. Because, even though the school holidays had only just started, Mrs Morris had a mere five minutes and thirty-nine seconds to spare every day, so it would take her a whole six weeks to hem a skirt.

But they were kind and caring, and might just have a trick or two up their sleeves.

Maisie Morris

"Maisie Morris, my precious poppet, will you please stop fidgeting before I stick pins into you instead of your skirt," said Mrs Morris. But because she had a mouthful of pins it sounded more like "Ayzee Orris, I recious ocket, ill use top idgeting afor I ftick tins in u..."

Maisie was standing on the wonky table in the tiny turret that she shared with her mother and was itching to get down. She was a small girl with huge eyes and a lot of fair hair that swooped out like a lampshade, and she looked exactly like Mrs Morris, only shorter and thinner. Once upon a time there had been a Mr Morris as well, but he had died in a freak accident with a vacuum cleaner two days after Maisie was born, which meant that Mrs Morris was a single mother. Now, single mothers get a lot of bad press these days, and some other mothers whisper

mean things about them in supermarkets and say them louder on chat shows.

"Oh, they spend all day in their dressing gowns eating crisps and reading horoscopes," say some people.

"I hear they force their children up chimneys for money," say others.

But Mrs Morris did none of these things. In fact, compared to most of the whispering mothers, she was a world champion supermum. She had not called her daughter anything ridiculous like Grinchy-pants or Barbarootie. She had not forced her to learn the dulcimer or Latin, and she had *never* made her wear flowery velvet dresses for tea on a Sunday.

"Oh, but the children are all gangsters who steal scooters and smoke cigars," whisper the other mums.

But Maisie was a bookish sort of girl who always ate her greens, did her homework and never smoked cigars. She was thrice winner of the St Regina's Primary prize for macramé owls and was the sort of girl who wore pants with days of the week sewn on and never got the day wrong.

And Maisie loved old people. She didn't mind if

they smelled a bit funny. She didn't mind that they always gave her stale boiled sweets covered in fluff; she didn't even mind when they fell asleep in their soup and had to have carrots washed out of their hair.

She loved Mr Nidgett, who was the father of Mr Nidgett Jr, who now ran Peabody and Nidgett's (which only stocked extra-large tweed suits and doilies). She loved Colonel Snell, who had a large waxed moustache and had once lived in India, where he had been in charge of the King George VIII Royal Emergency Gardening Battalion. She loved Minnow Rapsey, who had pushed a tin soldier so far up his nose as a boy that it got stuck behind his eye and stayed there for seventy-two years. She even loved Bristow Muldoon, who had only one leg and wore the same vest for weeks and mistook her for his awful niece Mavis who stole his liquorice comfits.

But best of all she loved Mrs Loveday Pink, who was the founder of the All-Groutley Over Fifty-Nine Under Five-Foot-Four Formation Ballroom Dancing Club. In her heyday she had won several trophies for her tango, and her lambada was legendary in Brentville. No one had a tighter dress, a whiter smile or a bigger hairdo than Loveday Pink. And although she was a lot older and bigger now and looked a bit like an overstuffed sequinned sausage, the overall effect was still superbly glamorous.

That morning Mrs Pink was going to teach Maisie the quickstep, which was why Maisie was so anxious to get off the table.

"Maisie, you know I love you to pieces, but will you *please* stop hopping around; your hem is wonky and my patience is thin," grumbled Mrs Morris, spitting half a dozen pins across the floor. "Whatever is the matter with you? Do you need the toilet?"

"No, Ma," said Maisie, wondering why mothers always think you need a wee when there is something urgent on your mind. "Mrs Pink's expecting me, and she says if I'm good enough I can enter the Groutley 'Let's Dance' Zinc Medallion competition."

Mrs Morris smiled sadly. "Oh, Maisie," she said. "It's a fair awful lot of time and money. You'll need special shoes and spangly tights; where am I going to get the money for all that palaver? You know I'd get you anything in the world if I could, except perhaps a pogo stick, because they are too dangerous and I don't understand them. But you'd have more chance asking Mrs Arkwright, who is as rich as Croesus but as stingy as Scrooge. Now come on, hop out of that skirt and run along. And don't let Mrs Arkwright catch you; you know the old people aren't allowed to dance."

"But why not?" she asked.

"For all the tea in Biggleswade I haven't the foggiest." Mrs Morris laughed. "But that's the way it is, lovey, and we have to like it if we want to keep our titchy tiny turret, don't we?"

"Yes, Ma," sighed Maisie, wriggling out of her skirt.

Mrs Morris grabbed her round the middle and plonked her down on the floor. "Go on," she said, giving her a big hug. "You don't want to keep Mrs Pink waiting."

Maisie yanked her trousers up, which were still round her ankles from the trying-on session, skipped out of the turret and clattered down the spiral stairs to the west wing.

Mrs Morris picked up the pins from the floor and trudged down to the scullery, where she would spend the next three hours hand-washing twenty

sets of dirty underwear with nothing but her bare
hands and a threadbare nail brush which was all Mrs
Arkwright would pay for.

The Rumpus Room

The rumpus room was the most poorly named room in Withering Heights. At least dining (in a manner of speaking) occurred in the dining room, and there were indeed beds in the bedrooms. But there was no rumpus to be heard in the rumpus room. That was because rumpus was firmly banned in Mrs Arkwright's numerous rules, as were hulla-balloo, pandemonium, cacophony and any other loud-sounding activity.

The only noise allowed was the television. The old people liked television, especially the phone-in programmes where well-groomed young doctors would solve all the problems of housewives from Sudbury and the like in thirty seconds flat. The old people liked solving the problems themselves.

"Oh, you don't want to do that," Mrs Hilditch would say, shaking her head. "You want to run away

with the fishmonger from Basildon."

When Maisie entered the room they were arguing over the correct way to stuff a chicken.

"Sausages and sage," said Minnow Rapsey, who was called Minnow because he was the youngest and smallest in his family; only now he was the oldest, but the name had somehow stuck.

"Giblets, just giblets," said Colonel Snell knowledgeably. "In India we used to hang the chickens for twenty days—"

But he was cut off abruptly by Mr Nidgett. "Enough, Snell! No more ghastly tales of imperial squalor."

"Hello," said Maisie, seizing her moment.

Twenty wrinkled faces swivelled round. "Hello, Maisie!" they chorused, their puckered-up mouths smiling madly.

"Doesn't she look lovely," said the Twitchett twins, Edith and Agatha, simultaneously.

"Oooh, adorable," agreed Hilda Higginbottom, spraying Jaffa Cake crumbs down her paisley polyester smock.

"Leave my liquorice comfits alone!" said Bristow Muldoon, slipping his sweets inside his sweaty vest.

"Hands off, all of you!" came a commanding voice from the corner. "She's all mine this morning."

Loveday Pink stood looking for all the world like a trapeze artist at a Help the Aged revue show. She was wrapped in a gold lamé tutu and on her head was an arrangement of feathers that looked like an exploding cormorant. Now this might not sound too out of the ordinary to you – for all I know you are this very minute dressed entirely in sky-blue crushed velvet loon pants. However, I can assure you that in a room full of cardigans and surgical stockings she stood out like a Christmas tree fairy in August.

"Hello, Mrs Pink," said Maisie politely. "I couldn't get any special shoes; will plimsolls be all right?"

"They'll be just dandy." Loveday smiled, looking down at Maisie's frayed dirty gym shoes. "How's your ma today? I hope Mrs Arkwright hasn't got her gutting bloaters again – she smelled like Billingsgate in a heatwave for a whole week after that. Frightful it was, frightful. Anyway, no need to worry about that old viper Mrs Arkwright; that halfwit husband of hers has driven her into Groutley to have her roots retouched in Burnished Llama at Brenda's Sooper

Sets – that'll cost a packet, I shouldn't wonder."
Loveday Pink disliked Mrs Arkwright as much as Mrs
Arkwright disliked her.

"Now," she said. "We've no proper dance music,
because Mrs Althrop's hands are too gippy to play
the piano and Mrs Arkwright has had the keys
removed, so there'd be precious little point anyway.
We'll just have to put on one of my old records."

Loveday heaved a battered old wind-up gramophone out from under her armchair. She cranked
the handle and it crackled into life.

"There we are," she said.

Maisie listened. It was a song she didn't recognize
but the old people seemed to.

"Oh, Johnny Sparkles, he's super!" said a lot of the
ladies.

"Lovely clean nails."

"Such a good head of hair."

Maisie was about to ask if it played more modern
music like at the Razzmatazz Roller Rink roller disco,
but before she could say "screaming habdabs" she
was whirling round and round the rumpus room
with Loveday Pink – past Colonel Snell; past Bristow
Muldoon and his liquorice; past the Twitchett twins,

who were singing at the tops of their voices, which was quite high up indeed.

"One-two-three, step-two-three, twirl-two-three," shouted Loveday Pink encouragingly but quite pointlessly as Maisie's feet were dangling in mid-air. It was wonderful; Maisie felt as if she were flying.

Mrs Arkwright on the other hand was not having nearly as much fun. In fact, she was positively fuming. Brenda of Brenda's Sooper Sets had had an accident with some super-grip curlers and a bottle of extra-strength setting lotion and was in bandages in Groutley General, leaving Mrs Arkwright with her roots showing and her temper fraying.

"What am I supposed to do? I'll have to wear a

scarf all week until that lazy twerp has got herself back to work. Why she can't work with second-degree burns is beyond me," she snapped to Trevor as they climbed back into their mint-green Fraud Console.

"That's right, my little vulture," humphed Mr Arkwright, who was also rather annoyed, as he had been planning to sneak off to the turf accountant's to place a bet on a horse called Beggar's Muddle that was in the three fifteen at Stewcaster, and didn't like having his plans rearranged over something as inconsequential as a hairdo.

"Back to Withering Heights then," said Mrs Ark-wright. "I'll just have to spend the morning painting my toenails."

And off they set. Which meant they arrived home just as the quickstep in the rumpus room reached a crescendo, with Maisie being tossed into the air for a full somersault, the Twitchett twins hitting top c and Mr Nidgett accidentally running his wheelchair into a vase of orange chrysanthemums.

"What in the name of Estée Lauder are those wretched wrinklies up to now!" fumed Cynthia as she threw her hamster fur coat onto the hall floor

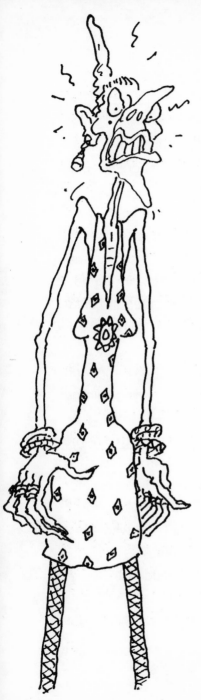

where Mrs Morris would have to pick it up later. "They think they can hoodwink me, having a party while I'm out facing a national disaster."

She stalked up the staircase towards the rumpus room, with Trevor following closely behind.

Mrs Arkwright was not best pleased at the sight that greeted her.

"Stop! Stop it at once!" she shrieked.

Loveday Pink and Maisie fell to the floor in shock, Mr Nidgett fell out of his wheelchair and the gramophone fell into the pool of water from the vase, causing Johnny Sparkles to gurgle and splutter.

"Maisie Morris," said Mrs Arkwright triumphantly, peering down at Maisie so that

Maisie could see right up her flaring nostrils. "I might have known you would be at the bottom of this, you idiotic midget. You think you're so clever with your saccharin smile, your shiny hair and your smooth skin. Well, you're not so clever this time! You're nothing more than a rotten little troublemaker, just like your useless mother. No wonder your daddy died – he was probably sick of you two twits."

Maisie's eyes filled with tears but she was determined not to cry in front of Mrs Arkwright. There was nothing Mrs Arkwright liked better than making her cry.

"Loveday Pink," snapped Mrs Arkwright, glaring furiously at Maisie's dancing partner. "The last thing I need after the morning I've had is a loony in a leotard. You have stepped your last fandango. One more rumba from you and you'll be locked in the hospital wing."

Maisie gulped and turned quite pale at the thought of poor Loveday being shut in the hospital wing. It was an awful place, freezing cold, dark and echoey. People who went in only left again when they were collected in a coffin by two tall thin grey undertakers called Grimwood and Bowdery.

"And as for you, Maisie Morris, get out of here at once and clean the toilets with your toothbrush; if I catch you in here again your mother will be out of a job and you will be in St Strangeway's Home for Horrible Girls faster than you can say 'Yves Saint Laurent'."

Maisie turned even paler. St Strangeway's Home for Horrible Girls was a large gloomy institution run by a band of pitiless military nuns called the Sisters of No Mercy. All the inmates had tattoos and really did smoke cigars, and Maisie definitely did not want to live there.

"And as for the rest of you vandals," added Mrs Arkwright, glowering at Mr Nidgett in particular, "no tea in your tea, no television and no Christmas. It's cancelled." And with that off she stamped in a cloud of meanness and revolting perfume.

Loveday pulled Maisie to her enormous bosom. "Don't you fret, Maisie Morris," she said. "We'll think of something."

"If only I were a bit bigger, I could give her what for," said Maisie, trying to be terribly brave but feeling very small and insignificant indeed.

Loveday held her even tighter. "Every town has

its miracles, Maisie, even Groutley."

It would certainly take a miracle to deal with Mrs Arkwright. And while Groutley might have looked as if a miracle hadn't so much as set foot there in a hundred years, you never knew when one might be lurking round the corner.

Gaston Regis
d'Angin Cummerbund

Maisie lay on the single bed, which, apart from a wonky table and a laundry basket, was the only furniture in the turret she shared with Mrs Morris. Mrs Arkwright had confiscated the other bed as punishment so Maisie now slept in the laundry basket. She had cleaned the toilets with her toothbrush until they sparkled but Mrs Arkwright was still seething, so Maisie was staying out of her way in case she accidentally started an over-enthusiastic beetle drive.

Instead she was reading one of her books. It was a plotty tale of schoolgirl derring-do in which the plucky heroine saves a drowning puppy, jumps a clear round in the gymkhana, puts her rather less attractive rival firmly in her place, organizes a super midnight feast and gets back to the dorm at St Semolina's just in time to avoid a ticking-off from

the firm but fair headmistress. She was just reaching the part where Tabitha Fotherington-Noble gets a detention for wearing non-regulation pants in an important lacrosse match against Custard Court, when she heard an enormous crash from the yard below.

By climbing onto the table and leaning forward so her head touched the glass, she could see the legs of Terry Perry, the delivery boy, sticking out from under an assortment of boxes and bags. Maisie liked Terry Perry enormously. He was in the top year at Groutley Comprehensive and could do terrific scissor kicks and cut a brick in half with his hand.

He'd learned that from his dad, who ran the Flash Legs Kung Fu video shop on Groutley High Street. Mrs Morris thought he should concentrate more on his A levels, but Maisie was too impressed with his karate tricks to care.

Maisie thought for a minute. No one would mind if she spoke to Terry Perry. Mrs Morris was busy boiling pigeon carcasses down for soup, Mr Arkwright was polishing his car and Mrs Arkwright was on her sunbed turning herself a delicate shade of orange. So she pulled on her shoes and headed down the spiral stairs to the tradesman's entrance.

"Hello, Maisie," said Terry as he wiped congealed tripe off his trousers. His bicycle and cart had crashed into the waste-disposal chute, down which all the leftovers came whizzing from the kitchen two floors above. "How's the old dragon?" he asked. "Did you know she's got a lizard's tail under her skirt and claws on her feet?"

Maisie giggled but secretly thought that he might actually be telling the truth.

"What are you doing here?" she asked, changing the subject quickly.

"Got a new one coming in, haven't you? I'm delivering his things." He pulled a piece of paper from his pocket. "Gaston Regis d'Angin Cummerbund. Funny old name that. Anyway, I'm in a hurry so you'll have to move these yourself. See you later, alligator!" And he sped off doing a wheelie which Maisie thought looked fantastically dangerous.

But far more interesting was the luggage that Terry had left behind. There were several swirly multicoloured boxes in different sizes, an enormous leather bag that had *Property GRDC* stamped on it and a long stick with a silver knob at one end and a hook at the other. Maisie was very interested in the stick; it looked like it could possibly be a riding crop and there was nothing she wanted more than a pony.

"It's a quangle stick," came a voice from behind her.

Maisie jumped and turned round.

The voice came from a small man, brown as a berry with a nearly bald head apart from white tufts at the side and whiskery sideburns, enormous

ears and dark eyes that
shone like blackcurrants.
He was dressed in a
beautiful velvet suit the
colour of an auber-
gine, and very shiny
shoes that were pointy
and turned up at the ends.
Under his arm was a large biscuit tin with holes in
the lid.

"It's for hunting quangle, of course." He nodded
at the stick, as if it were a stupid thing not to know.
"Allow me to introduce myself." He smiled. "Gaston
Cummerbund."

"Maisie Morris," said Maisie slowly, staring up in
wonder at the stranger. "What's a quangle?" she
asked.

"It's a fearsome creature, half puma, half chicken.
Hundreds of them stalk the forests of Perratootoo."

Maisie did not know what to say to this. So
she asked another question that was burning quite
sharply on her mind instead. "How did you get here?"

"Aha," said Mr Cummerbund. "That's a secret for
another day. Now, where is my room?"

Maisie knew that Mrs Arkwright was supposed to check all newcomers in so she could search their luggage for forbidden things and make sure they understood her rules and regulations. But Maisie also knew that not disturbing Mrs Arkwright when she was on her sunbed was one of those rules, so she decided that it would be better to get Mr Cummerbund inside before he caused a ruckus (which had also been banned after the ballroom dancing). So with two of his boxes balanced in her arms she led the way up the staircase.

Yam Restorer, Gastromancers and Monkey Onassis

M_r Cummerbund's room was dark with thick, dusty moth-eaten curtains and no carpet, but Mr Cummerbund didn't seem to mind and started unpacking immediately, whistling happily to himself. Maisie, who by rights should have gone back to her room by now, was too engrossed in the weird and wonderful objects Mr Cummerbund was pulling from his leather bag to leave.

Out came a large glass bottle with a cork stopper and a green label on the side that said: HANDLE WITH CARE – QUALIFIED USE ONLY. Inside, a lavender-coloured liquid fizzed and foamed most interestingly.

"What is it?" gasped Maisie.

"Yam restorer," said Mr Cummerbund.

"What's it for?"

"For restoring people who have accidentally been turned into yams," he said matter-of-factly.

"Does that happen often?" asked Maisie.

"Oh, in Outer Vulcania it happens at least once a month. Naughty children accepting sweets from strangers, then *wham*! Turned into a yam. Without this they'd just have to stay like it for ever, with a policeman to guard them from marauding vegetarians. Worse is when they only half turn. There was a half boy half yam living near the Limpopo for years before I came along. Just in time as well. His aunt was about to slow boil his arm for tea."

"Gosh!" said Maisie.

Next he pulled out a red shimmery belt with odd implements attached to little hooks.

"Coo," said Maisie. "What's that?"

"It's a gastromancer's belt. Don't tell me you've never heard of a gastromancer before!"

Maisie didn't think she had.

"A gastromancer is who you call when you've got an evil spirit in your house. They have big round tummies and sticky-out backsides, and when they find the evil spirit they hoover it right up their bottom and then you can talk to it in their tummy and tell it off."

Maisie secretly thought that anyone who walked

into Withering Heights and tried to hoover things up their bottom would get sent straight to Groutley Police Station, but she was too polite to say so.

Until this point Maisie had forgotten about the big biscuit tin with the holes that was on the floor next to her. But she was about to get very interested in it indeed. Because all of a sudden it started to rattle and move around.

"Stop that now," said Mr Cummerbund sternly to the tin.

The tin stopped. But the second Mr Cummerbund turned back to his unpacking it banged noisily across the floor, whereupon the lid fell off and a very bad-tempered monkey shot out.

Maisie yelped. The monkey spat at her.

"Oh, for heaven's sake," said Mr Cummerbund to the monkey. "My sincerest apologies," he said to Maisie, who was wiping monkey spit off her T-shirt. "He can be very trying when he's shut in for too long. But it's for his own good," Mr Cummerbund added pointedly to the monkey, who was scratching its messy fur and glaring at him.

"What is his name?" asked Maisie excitedly, who loved all animals, which – of course – she was banned from keeping at Withering Heights.

"His name is Monkey Onassis and he is an international jewel thief," said Mr Cummerbund. "Or at least he was until I caught him in the Doge of Caracus's palace and made him agree to stop it and be my helper, or face being sold for parts to a small specialized restaurant. As long as you hide shiny things and keep him shut in his tin on journeys, he's perfectly house-trained now."

Maisie wasn't so sure. Monkey Onassis seemed to be looking for fleas in his armpit.

"If Mrs Arkwright catches him she'll lock him in the cellar with the other pets," she said worriedly. "Mr Nidgett hasn't seen his parrot for years and the Twitchett twins are only allowed to see their dog, Jarvis, on their birthday for five minutes through the trapdoor."

"Hmm," thought Mr Cummerbund aloud. "Well, in that case you had better look after him in your room. You seem like a girl who won't let a monkey get stolen."

"Gosh, thanks," said Maisie. "Can I take him now?"

"Of course. And do come back tomorrow," he said, bowing slightly as he opened the door.

"I will," she promised. "I will."

Maisie carried the rather heavy Monkey Onassis up the rickety stairs. What a day it had been! But it wasn't over yet.

She had had her suspicions as to what Mrs Morris would say when she saw Monkey Onassis, and she was right.

"Lawks-a-mussy, Maisie! Lord knows, I know how

much you love all the creatures of the world, but what have I told you about bringing in strays from the street! Mrs Arkwright would have a purple apoplexy if she saw that fellow in here."

"But he's an international jewel thief, Ma," said Maisie.

"I don't care if he's Frank Sinatra," said Mrs Morris. "He can't stay in here and that is final. I'm sorry, sweetie, if I could I would let you keep an entire zoo in the scullery, but Mrs Arkwright is allergic to the sight of anything furry unless it's dead and in the form of a coat, and we wouldn't want that to happen, would we?"

Maisie reluctantly pushed a protesting Monkey Onassis back in his biscuit tin and was about to tramp back down the spiral stairs to Mr Cummerbund's room, when there was a crash and an awful lot of shouting and Mrs Arkwright started stamping up the other way. So Maisie put the tin in her laundry basket, slammed the lid shut and sat on it.

Mrs Arkwright had fallen asleep on the sunbed and had turned the exact colour of a Strawberry Mivvi. She was not happy.

"Marigold Morris, this is all your fault!" she shrieked at Maisie's mum. "Look at me! I have to go to the Groutley Gas-Fitters' Annual Fancy Dress Ball later, so you will have to spend the rest of the afternoon rubbing cream over me and hoping this colour fades to Bournemouth Bronze by teatime. And you had better not be hatching anything either," she said, eyeing Maisie suspiciously.

"Oh no, Mrs Arkwright," said Maisie as sincerely as she could muster.

"Yes, well..." said Mrs Arkwright. "Just don't even think about it."

She stamped back downstairs, Mrs Morris following behind with a large jar of Dr Potter's All-Purpose Soothing Liniment – good for sunburn, wasp stings, foot rot and chocolate stains.

Maisie breathed a sigh of relief and opened the laundry basket.

Monkey Onassis had eaten her pyjamas.

Tall Tales and Tricks

By the time she got back from dealing with Mrs Arkwright's sunburn, Mrs Morris had forgotten all about Monkey Onassis. And, as Mrs Morris spent so little time in the turret anyway, what with all the bottoms to polish, fish to gut and floors to scrub, Maisie thought she would keep him in her laundry basket, just for a little while. It meant she didn't get much sleep, as Monkey Onassis's manners were appalling and his personal hygiene levels left a lot to be desired as well. Not only did he insist on having Maisie's pillow, but he spent at least half the night pulling fleas out of his coat and eating them.

But Maisie was too excited to sleep properly anyway. She wondered where Mr Cummerbund came from and why he was here, and what other incredible objects he had in his bag.

After her ma had left she made herself a bowl

of Krispy Korny Flakes and gave Monkey Onassis a mugful which he ate by sticking his head in the mug and then throwing his face back, which meant rather a lot of cereal got on his fur and on the floor. "Hoop!" he said irritably. As she was only allowed baths on Wednesdays and Sundays and it was still Tuesday, Maisie had to wash him under the cold tap, which resulted in a minor flood and some loud squawking on the part of Monkey Onassis. Maisie thought she would ask Mr Cummerbund about monkey care later, but for now she was more interested in seeing what else he had brought to Withering Heights, so she put the bedraggled monkey back in the basket, shut the lid and hopped down the stairs.

Mr Cummerbund answered the door with a bow. "A pleasure to see you, Miss Morris," he said, waving her inside.

Maisie gasped; the room had been transformed. Instead of the bare floorboards there were patterned Persian rugs; on the walls were pictures of deserts and forests and other faraway places; orange lanterns glowed in every corner; and a huge globe spun slowly on a silver thread from the ceiling.

"Did you bring all this with you?" she asked, thinking that Terry Perry would never have made it all the way from Groutley Station to Withering Heights with all these things crammed in his wooden cart.

"In a manner of speaking," said Mr Cummerbund. "I conjured them up from memory, and you carry your memory everywhere you go; so, yes, I did bring them all with me."

"What do you mean, *conjured* them up?" she asked.

"Exactly that," said Mr Cummerbund. "Haven't you ever thought about ice cream so hard you could actually taste it?"

Maisie said she had thought about Marmite so hard once that she was nearly sick.

"Well, there you are," he said. "I just go one step further and make it appear in front of me."

Maisie was so excited she could hardly breathe. "Are you ... a wizard?" she whispered.

"That's a word I don't like to use," said Mr Cummerbund. "Every Tom, Dick or Harry goes round nowadays with a spangly stick and a pointy hat claiming to be a wizard. The whole trade has been downgraded terribly. Let's just say I have special powers."

"I've never met a wizard before," said Maisie. "My teacher Miss Stringfellow says magic isn't real; she says it's all mumbo-jumbo like ghosts and aromatherapy."

"Well, that's the problem, you see," said Mr Cummerbund. "When people grow up they stop believing in magic. That's what school is for – to make you think there's a rational explanation for everything. They tell you pigs can't fly – well, that's a load of rot for a start. I've seen several swarms of Gloucester Old Spot in my time, winging their way happily towards Dudley in a very impressive arrow formation. I tell you – question everything!"

"Could I be a wizard?" asked Maisie hopefully.

"Ha! A child being a wizard – imagine that! Absolutely not, far too dangerous for someone so small. But children can see magic that grown-ups can't."

"Oh," Maisie said, disappointed, having thought that maybe he had come to tell her she was to be his apprentice and give her a special cloak and hat. "Why are you here then?"

"Well, I'm getting old, of course. Why else would I be here?"

"Can't you just magic yourself young again?" asked Maisie, thinking that if she had magic powers she would never have to do anything she didn't want to.

"Well, it is possible – I do have a bottle of Egyptian age subtracter somewhere – but it's against all regulations. You see, if we all stayed young it would be awfully overcrowded with trickery in the world. We all have to retire some day."

"What will you do then?"

"Well, I shall do what all old people do – pretend to be deaf, play Burt Bacharach records too loudly and laugh at young people," he said. "But I shall always be ready for emergency wizardry. You know, if something is so colossal it needs a miracle to sort it out."

And he gave Maisie a wink.

Maisie saw it and gulped. Even Groutley has its miracles, she thought. But she dared not believe it was him. But then again. He was so unusual, so magnificent. Could it be? Maisie's tummy began to tingle with the thought.

"What sort of tricks can you do?" she asked, hopping from one foot to the other.

"I can do all sorts of things that would blow your socks off," he said, smiling. "Would you like to see?"

Maisie nodded, her eyes almost popping out of her head.

"Very well." And he picked Maisie up and sat her on what had been a very rickety wooden chair but was now a gold throne with red tasselled cushions, a mug holder and a television screen that shot out on a long arm and changed channel itself according to your mood.

The Flying Bed

"Now," said Mr Cummerbund. "Let me see. What do you want most in the whole world?"

"A pony," said Maisie quickly.

"Hmm. I'm not too good with large farm animals," he said. "They seem to get a bit mixed up on the way – last time I tried an ever-milking cow I ended up with a milkman from Harrogate and thirty-six pints of semi-skimmed. Something a little less alive, maybe."

Maisie was disappointed but thought that if hiding Monkey Onassis from Mrs Arkwright was tricky, then trying to cram a pony into the laundry basket as well was going to be very hard indeed. Then she got it.

"A bed," she said. Then Monkey Onassis could have the laundry basket to himself and happily scratch and eat fleas all night.

"Very well," said Mr Cummerbund. "Start thinking.

Close your eyes and think about the most amazing bed in the world."

Maisie thought very hard indeed.

Mr Cummerbund waved his hands in front of him. "Ala Zanussi!" he cried. Then *pow*! There was an enormous crack and a puff of smoke shot up from the floor.

Maisie opened her eyes and there it was. But this was no ordinary bed: Oh no. This was a gigantic four-poster affair with three mattresses, an exotic

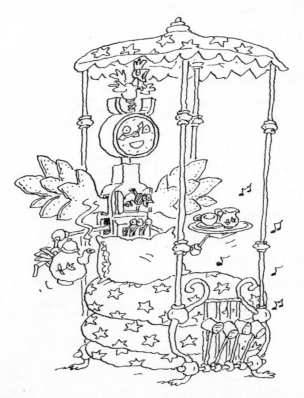

canary-feather eiderdown and a built-in alarm clock that gave you a choice of cockerel, cuckoo or Beethoven's Fifth, sang lullabies in twenty-seven different languages, made you tea and dispensed hot lemon-scented towels if you put a penny in a slot on the bedstead.

"What an excellent imagination," exclaimed Mr Cummerbund. "So lacking in many children today. They spend far too much time eating sweets and playing video games and not nearly enough time thinking. How can anything extraordinary happen to you if you have no imagination? But you, Maisie Morris, will go far."

Maisie was sure she hadn't thought about the towel dispenser, but, as Mr Cummerbund said, these things could get a little muddled on the way. Still, it was a truly fantastic bed.

It would certainly knock the smile off Belinda Braithwaite's face. Belinda, who was in Maisie's class at St Regina's, was a horrid spoiled show-off whose daddy had bought her a pony, skis, a skateboard, three kinds of sparkly earmuffs and a year's supply of rum and raisin ice cream all for one birthday. She was also very mean to Maisie. "Look at manky

Maisie in her second-hand skirt!" she would shriek. "Maisie's mum cleans toilets for a living – I bet she stinks like a toilet as well." And off she would skip with her equally awful friends, Lindy and Mindy, laughing and shouting, "Manky Maisie! Manky Maisie!" all the way.

Maisie hated Belinda, but she was not thinking too much about that at the moment. She was thinking about her new, marvellous bed.

There was just one problem.

"How will we get it back to the turret?" she asked. She was hardly going to get away with wheeling a four-poster bed through Withering Heights, particularly as it had started playing the "Battle Hymn of the Republic" very loudly.

"That's easy," said Mr Cummerbund. "Climb on board!"

Maisie hopped off the gold throne and Mr Cummerbund picked her up and swung her onto the bed, which was very high up indeed, and then climbed aboard beside her.

"Now hold tight and think about where you want the bed to go," he said.

Maisie thought about the little turret, hoping that

Mrs Morris was not currently in there, because there was a good chance of her getting squished.

"Ala Datsun!" cried Mr Cummerbund.

A strange sensation came over Maisie, a sort of electricity that started in her feet and crackled all the way to her ears. Then *whoosh*! In a split second they had left Mr Cummerbund's room and arrived in another. But it wasn't the turret. Instead they had arrived in the dining room just as Mrs Morris was serving up cabbage water for lunch.

"Oops!" said Maisie. At the last minute her tummy had rumbled and she had thought about lunch by mistake.

It was quite a kerfuffle. The Twitchett twins applauded; Mr Nidgett woke up from his bowl; and Loveday Pink, who was wearing a peacock feather batwing ballgown and a turban, gave Maisie, who had landed just behind her, an enormous hug.

Even Mrs Morris was impressed by her daughter's arrival.

"Glory be, Maisie!" she cried. "What in the name of immaculate contraptions have you got there?"

"It's my new bed," said Maisie. "Mr Cummerbund magicked it for me."

"Oooh, crikey, it's a wondrous thing, isn't it? I don't suppose even the Queen of London has one like this," said Mrs Morris, pulling a lever on one of the bedposts, which handed her a cup of hot cocoa and a Bourbon biscuit. But then she sighed. "I'm sorry, Maisie; it's very clever I'm sure, but rules are rules and Mr Cummerwhatsit is going to have to magic it straight back again before Mrs Arkwright has all our guts for garters."

But Mr Cummerbund was more interested in the soup. "Is that all these poor people have to eat?" he asked. "No wonder they have no zing in their step, no pizzazz in their perambulations. We must see to that at once."

"Coo, what's he going to do?" asked the Twitchetts.

"Right, everyone. Think about what you really fancy for lunch," said Mr Cummerbund, waving the soup ladle in the air. "Fish and chips maybe, or a big juicy cheesecake."

"Mercy me," said Mrs Morris. "Have you got a licence for this sort of thing?"

"Don't worry, Ma," said Maisie. "It'll be fine; just watch."

66

Mrs Morris wasn't so sure, but before she could get her ladle back Mr Cummerbund had shouted, "Ala Magimix!", an enormous puff of smoke had come out of the table, two old ladies had wet themselves and Mr Nidgett had singed an eyebrow.

But when the smoke cleared, on the table was the most fantastic feast you could imagine.

There were steaks and sausages, kidneys in aspic, long green fingery asparagus spikes, a whole pig's head with an orange in its mouth, jellies and junkets, fish paste sandwiches, a sherry trifle, jam tarts and custard, biscuits, three enormous turbots, five kinds of ice cream and a bag of liquorice comfits (that was all Bristow Muldoon ever thought about).

67

"Gosh," said Maisie.

"Superb," said Colonel Snell. "When we were in India all we had to eat were dung beetles and pickled herring."

"Shut up," said all the old people.

Mrs Morris was flummoxed. "Well!" She laughed. "I'm not sure I approve of all this tomfoolery. But it's about time these poor people had a decent dinner. I just hope he can magic the washing-up," she added, smiling at Mr Cummerbund.

Lunch was a resounding success. Mr Nidgett ate a whole roast duck; Loveday Pink had three helpings of her favourite lemon meringue pie; and Minnow Rapsey managed four curried eggs, three pork chops, two bowls of mulligatawny and a blanc-mange made of raspberries.

And when they were done, Mr Cummerbund cleared the table and did the washing-up in a spectacular way involving a lot of foam and invisible brushes. Then he stacked it up neatly and did some party tricks with a rabbit and Mrs Hilditch's hanky while Maisie used her bedstead to dispense lemon-scented towels to everyone using Colonel Snell's penny collection, which he kept in a jam jar hidden in his old King George VIII Royal Emergency Gardening Battalion trunk.

Mrs Morris was enjoying herself no end, but after Mr Nidgett fell asleep on the table for the third time she decided it was all quite enough high jinks for one day and they were to thank their lucky stars that Mrs Arkwright hadn't decided to pay them a visit.

"Now, Maisie," said Mrs Morris, "you must get this pantechnicon into the bedroom at once, and no more mischief from either of you. There's a mysterious blockage in Mr Nidgett's U-bend, so I shall be up to my armpits all afternoon and I don't want to be chasing about after you two."

Maisie and Mr Cummerbund promised to play gin rummy all afternoon with Loveday Pink in her bedroom as soon as they had dropped the bed off in the turret.

But in all the excitement Maisie had forgotten about Monkey Onassis.

Monkey Onassis and the Diamond Solitaire

While Maisie was conjuring up her great automatic all-singing bed, Monkey Onassis was getting up to his own mischief. Angry at being left behind, he had spent the morning fiddling with things in the turret. So far he had unscrewed two of the legs on the wonky table, pushed several pairs of Maisie's socks down the plughole of the sink, eaten a whole box of indigestion tablets and picked most of the putty out of the window surround, sending the pane of glass crashing onto the concrete several storeys down, which amused Monkey Onassis greatly.

But now he was beginning to get bored. And when Monkey Onassis got bored there was nothing he liked better than to search for diamonds. So he opened the turret door and padded stealthily down the spiral stairs.

The first place he arrived at was Colonel Snell's room. Luckily Colonel Snell, along with all the other old people, was busy in the rumpus room watching a documentary about head shrinkers in Patagonia.

Monkey Onassis sniffed. He couldn't smell diamonds. All he could smell was coal tar soap and cough sweets. But perhaps this was a cover-up! So Monkey Onassis started searching.

First he stuck his hand down the back of Colonel Snell's armchair, a dark and interesting crack which was just the sort of place to hide a diamond. Monkey Onassis found a limited edition King 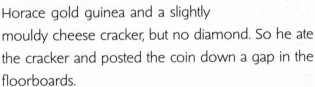 Horace gold guinea and a slightly mouldy cheese cracker, but no diamond. So he ate the cracker and posted the coin down a gap in the floorboards.

Next he rummaged through Colonel Snell's enormous King George VIII Royal Emergency

Gardening Battalion trunk. In it he found a trowel, a hoe, a do-it-yourself table-top combine harvester, a pair of secateurs and some slug pellets, but no diamond. He ate the slug pellets, which tasted of old burned rubber, jammed the hoe up the chute of the combine harvester and took the secateurs, which he thought might come in useful for cutting things later.

By now Monkey Onassis was getting annoyed at the lack of diamonds in Colonel Snell's room. So, without bothering to clean up the mess he had made, he hopped out of the door and went further down the corridor.

In Mr Nidgett's room he found two dozen antimacassars and a banana, but no diamond. He ate half the banana and stamped on the rest, which felt nice and squishy between his toes.

In the Twitchett twins' room he found a musical soap dish, a packet of lavender-flavoured lozenges, a book about bees and a pair of fancy sunglasses, but no diamond. He fiddled with the soap dish so that it played "Amazing Grace" backwards in a high, tinny sort of way.

In the garage he found several bunches of keys. Monkey Onassis liked keys very much. But he couldn't hold Colonel Snell's secateurs and the keys at the same time because it wouldn't leave him any hands to hunt diamonds with; so he put the secateurs in the darkest hole he could find, which happened to be the exhaust pipe of Mr Arkwright's mint-green Fraud Console. Then, clutching the keys, he let himself out of the garage and into Mr and Mrs Arkwright's rooms.

He sniffed the air, and smiled.

Now, most people would not be able to smell anything beyond the combination of Mrs Arkwright's rotten perfume and Mr Arkwright's extra-strong foot powder. But Monkey Onassis was a highly trained professional and he could detect a diamond in a dung heap. And there was no mistaking the smell in the Arkwrights' bedroom. It was twenty-four carat diamond. He began to search.

Under the bed he found a hosepipe (stolen from the not-so-famous Hosepipe Museum by Mr Arkwright so that he could sell it back to them at twice the price), a bottle of treacle-toffee-flavoured liqueur, hidden by Mrs Arkwright, and a glossy magazine full of articles like "Will Russet Rose hair colour make me a better person?" and "How my macaque-fur slippers made me the most popular hostess in town".

In the en suite luxury bathroom he found a very interesting jar of aquamarine-coloured bath salts, which foamed fantastically when he poured them down the toilet; and a pair of gold taps attached to the whirlpool bath, which he detached and sent the same way as the bath salts.

74

Monkey Onassis was just beginning to get annoyed when he saw a shiny wooden box sitting on top of the wardrobe. His eyes sparkled. A box was just the sort of place where a diamond might be hidden. And it was.

Inside Mrs Arkwright's jewellery box was a big flashy diamond solitaire ring. Monkey Onassis held it up to his eye and a kaleidoscope of colours spangled on the walls as the sunlight hit the egg-shaped jewel.

"Hoop!" he said excitedly, and, still clutching his keys, he took himself and the diamond back past the Twitchett twins, who were listening intently to their backward-playing musical soap dish in case it was sending messages from outer space; past Mr Nidgett, who had skidded on the banana mash in his wheelchair and fallen face down on the bed, where he had promptly gone to sleep; past Colonel Snell's room, where he was busy trying to remove the hoe from his combine harvester; and up the spiral staircase to the turret.

He was a little confused at first as, in his absence, a gigantic bed had somehow been squashed inside Maisie's bedroom and was singing "Hush-a-Bye, Baby" in Mandarin. But Monkey Onassis was tired from the diamond hunt; so, after posting the ring and keys through a hole in his biscuit tin, he climbed back into the laundry basket and settled down to pull fleas from his fur contentedly.

Boris Kalashnikov

It happened at teatime.

Mr Arkwright was parading in front of the en suite bathroom mirror in a new nylon shirt the colour of farm slurry. His hair shone with brilliantine and he looked as slippery as a cable-channel newsreader. He was just practising his "impress the ladies" simultaneous smile and wink when an almighty shriek came from next door.

"Trevor, come quick! We've been robbed, burgled, broken into, ransacked, pillaged!"

"What is it, my little triffid?" Mr Arkwright asked wearily, peering round the door.

Mrs Arkwright was dressed in a georgette frock the colour of a dead salmon, with a hairdo dyed to match. She was waving her jewellery box about like a whirling dervish.

"Look!" she squawked. "Clean gone, it is. My

diamond solitaire. Vanished! How am I ever going to show my face at the Groutley Glee Club Dancearama without it? Everyone will think we're poor!"

"Don't be ridiculous! How could a burglar have got in?" exclaimed Mr Arkwright.

"It must have been one of those evil circus dwarfs," said Mrs Arkwright. "Shinned up the drainpipe. Or one of those pygmy people from Outer Mongolia. Or a cat burglar slunk in through the window. Or leprechauns from Limerick come to terrorize me with their awful green faces and bad dress sense!"

"Or a nasty little blonde girl who is always up to no good," said Mr Arkwright triumphantly.

"That's it, Trevor!" cried Mrs Arkwright. "That revolting Morris maverick. I always knew she was a bad one. She gets it from her mother. I bet she's in cahoots with Loveday Pink as well. That overdressed octogenarian is always dripping with cheap costume jewellery. She must have had her eye on my ring and sent the brat in through the window to fetch it for her."

"Well, they can't have gone far," said Mr Arkwright. "The gates are locked. They must still be in Withering

Heights. Follow me." And off he set at a tremendous pace to find Loveday Pink and Maisie, with Mrs Arkwright teetering on her alpaca-skin stilettos behind him.

"There they are!" cried Mr Arkwright as they burst through the door of Loveday Pink's bedroom. "They've got another accomplice with them and they're gambling as well!"

Maisie, Loveday Pink and Mr Cummerbund looked up in shock from their gin rummy.

"Hello, Mr Arkwright," said Maisie. "We aren't gambling; we're playing quietly with absolutely no hullabaloo at all."

"Shut up, you varmint," said Mrs Arkwright. "I'll deal with you later. Now, where is it?" She glared at Loveday Pink. "Come on, you pinching pensioner – give me back my diamond ring immediately!"

"I don't know what you are talking about," said Loveday Pink haughtily. She did not like her gin rummy disturbed, particularly when she was winning.

"Yes, we've been in here all afternoon," said Maisie.

"I've told you once already – keep your trap shut," snapped Mrs Arkwright. "Or I will shut it for you with superglue."

"Leave the child alone," said Mr Cummerbund.

Mrs Arkwright looked at the stranger. In all the comings and goings, Mr Cummerbund had still not been checked in officially.

"And who exactly are you?" she demanded.

"My name is Gaston Regis d'Angin Cummerbund. I live in room 3B," he said.

"Poppycock!" said Mrs Arkwright. "I've never seen you before in my life; you are obviously the ring-leader."

"He's not," said Maisie. "He's a lovely man."

"Utter rot," said Mrs Arkwright. "And for the last time, shut up. No one is remotely interested in what you have to say."

"I can't see it, Cynthia," said Mr Arkwright, who had turned the room upside down during the shout-ing. "The child must have hidden it somewhere else – they'll have given it to her because the police would never suspect a schoolgirl."

"It's probably in her titchy tiny turret," said Mrs Arkwright. "Her mother will collect it later and send it off to a pawnshop with that daft delivery boy. Oh, they've got it all planned." Mrs Arkwright's imagination, which usually worked at a snail's pace, was running away with her.

"To the turret!" cried Mr Arkwright. "And you lot can come too – we don't want you calling any more of your gang and planning an escape."

So off trooped Mr and Mrs Arkwright, Maisie, Loveday Pink and Mr Cummerbund up the spiral stairs to the titchy tiny turret.

82

"What in the name of Max Factor is that monstrosity doing?" asked Mrs Arkwright. Maisie's new automatic bed was taking up most of the room. "Bought that with your ill-gotten gains, did you?"

Maisie didn't say anything. She didn't see the point as firstly she had been told to shut up three times, and secondly Mrs Arkwright would probably have been even more angry about the magic spells.

"Nothing to say for yourself, eh?" said Mr Arkwright. "Clear sign of guilt. Cynthia, call the police at once."

But Mrs Arkwright was not listening. She had picked up the biscuit tin lying on the bed and was shaking it. It clanked.

She ripped off the lid and screeched with delight. "I knew it! Here it is!" she said. On her finger was the missing diamond.

"And those are my car keys too!" said Mr Arkwright. "Planning a getaway, were you?"

Maisie couldn't hold her tongue any longer. "I don't know where they came from," she said. "Honestly, I've never seen either of them before. What would I want with a ring? And I can't drive yet; I can't even ride a bicycle."

"A likely story," said Mrs Arkwright. "You're as guilty as Guy Fawkes. And you know what happens to little juvenile delinquents like you, don't you?" she added scarily.

"They go to St Strangeway's Home for Horrible Girls?" asked Maisie.

"Oh no," said Mrs Arkwright. "St Strangeway's is far too good for the likes of you, you stunted sneak.

I've got something *much* more interesting in store for you and the rest of your revolting gang. I'm going to call Boris Kalashnikov."

"Who's Boris Kalashnikov?" whispered Maisie.

"He is the infamous head torturer of a particularly ruthless group of Russian pirates and is wanted in twenty-five countries for deeds of such barbarity they'd make your teeth fall out just thinking about them." She smiled a nasty smile. "First he will bend your arms the wrong way until they snap and you look like a loony. Then he will grate the soles of your feet with a cheese grater and make you eat the shavings."

Maisie was turning green.

"He will let rats nibble your ears and worms wriggle up your nostrils. And then he will scrape his nails down a blackboard so hard you'll wish the rats would hurry up and eat your ears clean off."

"How do you know him?" asked Loveday Pink suspiciously.

Mr Arkwright stepped forward. "Boris Kalashnikov is my evil twin brother."

This was in fact true. Boris's real name was Percy Arkwright but he had changed it because he thought Boris sounded more villainous, which it does. He was so bad he made Mr Arkwright look positively benevolent. He had an enormous black beard and a temper as filthy as his overgrown fingernails.

Maisie gulped.

"And when he's done," continued Mrs Arkwright, "I'm going to call Reg Yonkers from the council and have you transferred to St Strangeway's, by which point you will be so twisted and ugly the nuns will have to lock you in a cellar so you don't frighten the other girls. And I'll ask him to find you two fiends somewhere equally awful as well," she added, flashing her eyes angrily at Loveday Pink and Mr Cummerbund. "And as for Mrs Morris, she will have her wages halved and her hours doubled. Not that she'll be able to complain, because her teeth will have fallen out, if not her arms as well.

"Tonight, though, you will all be locked in here where you can't get up to any more criminal activity, as I am due at the Groutley Glee Club Dancearama in fifteen minutes and I don't want to miss pineapple on sticks and elaborate cocktails on your account. You can tell your mother that she can sleep in the scullery with the dirty washing and cockroaches."

And Mrs Arkwright whirled out of the room with Mr Arkwright in tow, locking the door behind her.

Mrs Arkwright's Soul

Maisie sat on the bed in between Mr Cummerbund and Loveday Pink. A big tear rolled slowly down her cheek.

"Now now, Maisie," said Loveday, giving her hand a squeeze. "You mustn't cry. It's not your fault that she is such a horror."

"Mrs Pink's right, you know," agreed Mr Cummerbund. "There are already too many tears in the world. Why, in London seventeen thousand five hundred and sixty-seven litres of tears are cried every day – that's why the River Thames is so enormous, carrying off all that sadness to the sea. Any more tears and we shall all be flooded."

Maisie managed a small smile but she was still very upset.

"The trouble with Mrs Arkwright," continued Mr Cummerbund, "is that she's got no soul."

"What's a soul?" asked Maisie, sniffing.

"A soul is a small and slippery organ, like a sliver of soap. It is quite see-through and doctors can never quite find it. But it is very important – it is what makes you feel all delicious and warm and tingly in your belly when you are happy."

"What has happened to Mrs Arkwright's soul?" asked Maisie.

"I don't think she ever had one to start with," said Mr Cummerbund. "What Mrs Arkwright has is a big black empty hole, all rotten and no use to anyone. And over the years that hole has just got bigger and bigger."

Maisie imagined the big black hole inside Mrs Arkwright. She would very much like to see it. But at that point someone else came up the turret stairs, interrupting her thoughts very loudly indeed.

Mrs Morris was white as a sheet, not that Maisie could tell because she was locked out on the stairs. "Crikey O'Reilly, Maisie," she said through the keyhole of the turret door. "I thought I told you to pack that magic lark in and play cards nicely."

"I did, Ma, honestly."

"Lordy, as if I haven't got enough to worry about, what with Mr Nidgett's U-bend and those Twitchett twins thinking aliens are in their soap dish. On top of that, someone seems to have jammed Colonel Snell's combine harvester and it's ploughed up the raffia bathroom mat, causing a right tangled mess. Now some Russian pirate is going to string us up on a blackboard and shave our feet or something." Mrs Morris was hysterical. "First of all you bring that hairy horror home in a biscuit tin, and then a singing bed lands in my cabbage soup. Honestly, Maisie, you know I love you, but it's enough to give anyone the heebie-jeebies."

"That's it!" said Maisie. "Monkey Onassis."

She opened the lid of the laundry basket. Monkey Onassis opened one eye and grumbled. He was still sleepy after his heist and did not take kindly to being woken up.

"Maisie," continued Mrs Morris through the keyhole, "you are the most precious thing in the whole world to me, but if I hear any more about simian shenanigans, I'll likely lose my marbles completely and have to be locked up in a straitjacket and eat nothing but jelly for the rest of my life, even before that Russian pirate gets his hands on me."

"No, Ma," said Maisie, ignoring Monkey Onassis's scrabbling and squawking, and hauling him out of his bed. "Monkey Onassis is an international jewel thief. He must have stolen the ring and brought it here for safe keeping."

"That's right!" said Mr Cummerbund, glaring at Monkey Onassis. "He is a devilish little fellow."

"Hoop!" argued Monkey Onassis.

"All we have to do is show him to Mrs Arkwright and she'll know I'm innocent!" said Maisie.

"But she'll lock him up," said Loveday Pink. "Or, worse, turn him into a fur hat and slippers. We can't have that."

Neither Maisie nor Monkey Onassis looked very happy at this prospect.

"I'm sure I can think of something," said Mr Cummerbund.

"Yes, well, you had better because I don't want my arms snapped by that Boris Clickety-Clack person and I don't think you do either," said Mrs Morris.

"But no more tomfoolery or jiggery-pokery, Maisie," she added. "And no escaping on that flying bed of yours. That thing is to stay in there until breakfast or you can bet your bottom dollar Mrs Arkwright will think of something worse – not that there could be such a thing."

"Yes, Ma," said Maisie.

"Good. Well, goodnight, my treasure. Now I am off to sleep in the scullery, and like as not I shan't get a wink, what with the cockroaches and who knows what else."

Mrs Morris stamped downstairs.

"What are we going to do?" cried Maisie. "We can't hand Monkey Onassis over or he'll be turned into accessories. And we can't use my bed to escape or Ma will send me to St Strangeway's herself, and I shall have to smoke cigars and chew gum even in lessons and I'll never see any of you again."

Monkey Onassis was looking very sorry for himself indeed. He puffed himself out and clutched his knees in a sad way. But as he shuffled, something jangled onto the floor.

It was a key. Monkey Onassis had not posted all of them into the tin. But it was not an ordinary-looking key. It was very spindly and unusual.

"By Jove!" said Mr Cummerbund slowly. "The little sneak has done something right! It's a skeleton key – it must open all the doors in Withering Heights."

"Coo," said Maisie. She had never heard of a skeleton key before.

"Excellent work," said Mr Cummerbund, patting Monkey Onassis on the head. "That way we can get out of here without using your bed, which means you won't have to use any magic at all, so Mrs Morris can't get frantic. Now, what we're going to do is give that bitter old battleaxe a taste of her own medicine."

Maisie thought of all the awful things she would like to do to Mrs Arkwright. She would like to teach her a lesson. Put a spanner in her works. Shut that rotten trap up for good. Something to really make her squirm. But what? She would like to put her in the giant washing tub and rinse her nastiness out. Then push her through the mangle in the scullery until she was as thin as paper and post her to Kathmandu.

"What is Mrs Arkwright frightened of?" asked Mr Cummerbund.

Maisie thought. "I don't think she's scared of anything."

"Oh, everyone is scared of something. Why, in Zanzibar I met a man who was scared of the letter h. He wouldn't have anything with that letter in his home – only he didn't have a home or a house; he had a bungalow. No h, you see. No hearth, no heating, no hot water, no hems on the curtains, no hankies, no ham. No happiness."

Maisie thought again. Then it came to her. Oh, it was a wonderful idea.

"We need to make her look old," she said.

"What's that?" asked Mr Cummerbund.

"We need to make her look old," said Maisie again. "That's what she's really frightened of. Looking old would scare her the most."

"It's true!" said Loveday. "Why, she's awfully vain. She would sooner have her face stretched until it's on the back of her head and she could see behind her than let it get crinkly."

"Well then, that's what we shall do." Mr Cummerbund laughed. "We shall make her older than Methuselah. We shall make her bottom sag and her eyelids droop and a big moustache grow on her lip."

He picked Maisie up and whirled her around.

"But how?" gasped Maisie.

"Wait and see," said Mr Cummerbund, his eyes shining like blackcurrants. "Wait and see."

Mrs Arkwright's Cabinet

Mrs Arkwright's bathroom cabinet was packed full of mysterious treatments in packets and tubes of every colour you could imagine. There were pills to make your hair grow in one place and creams to stop it growing in another. There were tonics and treatments to wake you up and ones to put you to sleep again. There was a bottle of wonderful pink liquid which promised to give you skin as soft as a baby's bottom, and a pot of something which claimed to contain extract of babies' bottoms.

Maisie looked up and down the shelves as Mr Cummerbund picked up the packets in turn. They had left Monkey Onassis shut in his tin under the iron grip of Loveday Pink, who had been only too pleased to monkey-sit for an evening.

"It beats listening to Colonel Snell talking about stealth parsnips," she had said.

Monkey Onassis had tried to say something too but his hooping had been muffled by Loveday Pink's ample backside.

"Eau de toilette," said Mr Cummerbund, looking at a tall bottle of pale yellow liquid with squiggly gold writing on the label. "Why would anyone want to smell like a toilet?"

Maisie didn't know.

"Now, let me see. We need to make sure it's something she uses every day. What do you reckon, Maisie?"

Maisie thought. "Vitamin pills," she said. "I know because she makes Ma buy her a new jar every week, so she must use an awful lot."

"Very well then. Now, which one is it?" mused Mr Cummerbund, peering at the pots and packets. "Aha!" He pulled out a jar of enormous yellow pills. *"Neville Swinglehurst's Revitalizing Vitamins,"* he read. *"Turn your shrivelled prune into peaches and cream. Take two a day. (Also good for tapeworm infestations.)* That must be it."

"What are you going to do?" asked Maisie. "Ma said there was to be no magic."

"No, Maisie, your ma said *you* were not to do any

magic, and you're not. *I* will be the one doing the magic. Besides, I don't expect she'd mind if a whole troop of sorcerers moved into Withering Heights when she sees what a whopping fantastical thing I am going to do."

He held the jar of pills out in front of him. "Ala Nintendo!" he cried.

A small pop came from inside and the pills jumped and twitched for a second.

"There we go," he said with satisfaction. "All done."

"But it doesn't look any different," said Maisie.

"Of course not," said Mr Cummerbund. "We don't want her to get suspicious. It's what's on the inside that counts."

"That's what Ma always says," said Maisie.

"And she's quite right too. Now come along, before those horrors get back from their outing."

And Mr Cummerbund led Maisie back out of the bathroom, up the stairs and into the turret, where Monkey Onassis gave a hoop of joy at being let out of his tin. Loveday Pink had underestimated the width of her backside and had unwittingly blocked most of his air holes.

Downstairs Mr and Mrs Arkwright arrived back from the Groutley Glee Club Dancearama in a foul mood and a taxi.

"Trevor, I am going straight to bed," snapped Mrs Arkwright. "Never in my life have I been so embarrassed. That car exhaust exploding all over Petunia Braithwaite's lemon organza twinset. And when those secateurs shot out and knocked Barry Trotter over like a bowling pin, I thought I would die on the spot. No doubt we shall be barred from Groutley Glee Club and sent to Coventry to boot."

Mr Arkwright was nonplussed. "I don't understand it," he said. "That car's only just been serviced."

"Next time book yourself in as well. There's clearly something missing." And Mrs Arkwright slammed the bathroom door shut.

"Stupid Maisie," she muttered to herself as she yanked off her false eyelashes. "And that dull mother of hers as well. Well, the sooner I get rid of the pair of them the better. And then I shall send for Grimwood and Bowdery and get them to cart all those awful old people off to the funeral parlour."

"They're not dead yet," said Mr Arkwright, who was lurking outside the door because he needed a wee urgently.

"Well, they jolly well will be when I have finished with them," said Mrs Arkwright, Sello-taping her cheeks back angrily. "And then I shall turn Withering Heights into a beauty farm and all my guests will be gorgeous and young. Only not as gorgeous as me," she added, admiring herself in the mirror.

"Now, where are my vitamins?"

She rummaged through the cabinet shelves. "Aha, there you are. Couldn't do without you, could I? Or I'd be as ugly as Loveday Pink."

She popped two yellow pills into her mouth and swallowed hard. Then she switched the light off and went to bed, leaving Trevor to wee in the dark. As he went to pick up his toothbrush his hand knocked the vitamin jar over, spilling some into the sink.

"Damn," he said. Not wanting to put the light on and upset Mrs Arkwright, he swished them down the plughole.

As he went to screw up the jar again a thought came over him and he shook out two pills onto his hand.

Can't do any harm, he thought. Maybe I'll wake up looking like a film star.

And so he gulped them down, let out a revolting belch and went to bed.

ReVenge

"Morning, Trevor," said Mrs Arkwright from under her airline flight mask, which she wore to keep out the light so as not to disturb her beauty sleep. "Time to get up. Boris will be here any minute and you know he hates to be kept waiting when there's torturing to be done. Then we have to call the workmen to turn Withering Heights into a top-class beauty retreat complete with Parisian make-up artists, Swedish massage parlours and Dungeness mud – I hear it's super for fatty deposits. Trevor! Are you listening?"

Trevor was trying to speak but his mouth didn't seem to want to move. Instead he just gurgled.

"What is the matter with you? You sound like one of those awful old people upstairs. Honestly, I worry about you sometimes." And she lifted up the flap of her mask to eye him in a nasty manner.

She did not expect the sight she was greeted with.

"Aaaaaagghhhhh!" she shrieked, pointing at the frightful creature beside her.

"Aaaagggggh!" went Trevor, pointing back.

This went on for several minutes before both of them realized that they should take a look at themselves. They fought to get into the bathroom first, both squeezing through the door at once, and then they looked in the mirror.

"AAAAAAAAAGGGGGGGGGGGHHHHHHHHHH!" they screamed together.

"What's happened?" sobbed Mrs Arkwright. "I look like a … a *granny*."

"So do I," cried Mr Arkwright.

And they did. Overnight the pills had worked their magic. Their faces were as lined and droopy as a bloodhound's; their hair had fallen out; and their teeth, what was left of them, were black and wonky. They looked like ghouls from the London Dungeon.

"Maybe it's not that bad. Maybe other people won't notice," said Mr Arkwright hopefully.

"Of course it's that bad!" shouted Mrs Arkwright. "I'll be the laughing stock of Groutley. I'll never be able to show my face in the bingo hall again."

"Maybe we can cover it up a bit," suggested Mr Arkwright.

"What with?" screamed Mrs Arkwright. "Carrier bags? It's that Maisie Morris again. I know it. She must be behind it. She's a witch, a warlock, a brazen little troublemaker. Well, I'll show her."

She flew out of the bedroom, with Mr Arkwright in what would have been hot pursuit, but what, now he had arthritis and ingrown toenails to contend with, not to mention needing to wee every few minutes, was more like a snail's crawl.

On the way she crashed into Mrs Morris, who was tramping up the stairs to start serving porridge.

Mrs Morris screamed when she saw her. "Oh, my giddy stars! It's the mummy of Tooting Common come to take us all back to the pyramids."

"No it isn't, you imbecile, it's Mrs Arkwright, and you had better come with me this instant," said the apparition.

"Lawks-a-mussy! What has happened to you?" asked Mrs Morris.

"Maisie Morris is what has happened," snapped Mrs Arkwright. "And I am going to sort her out once and for all." And with that she burst into the turret.

Maisie's eyes nearly popped out of her head and her mouth hung open. She had never seen anything like it. Mrs Arkwright looked a hundred years old.

"Two hundred, actually," said Mr Cummerbund, who could tell what she was thinking, which was an awfully useful trick to have.

Maisie tried to shut her mouth but couldn't as she was still marvelling at the monster in front of her.

"What have you done, you awful child?" screamed Mrs Arkwright.

"But ... nothing. I..." stammered Maisie, not wanting to lie but not wanting to tell the whole truth either.

"A likely story," said Mrs Arkwright. "She's nothing but a big fibber."

At this point, the old people, having been disturbed by the shouting, came up the stairs to see what was happening.

"Gosh, Mrs Arkwright, you look awfully peaky. Doesn't she, Agatha?" said one of the Twitchett twins.

"Oooh, and Mr Arkwright too!" said the other twin.

Mr Arkwright had finally managed to creak up

the stairs, still in his pyjamas.

"What's happening?" shouted Mr Nidgett, who was stuck on the landing because his wheelchair couldn't climb up the turret stairs.

"Mr and Mrs Arkwright have lost their hair and teeth somewhere," shouted Colonel Snell. "Do you want me to hunt them down?" he added to Mrs Arkwright. "I'm a devil of a tracker. In India I could find a—"

But he was cut off by all the others, who shouted, "Shut up!"

"We don't need them hunting down, you mental military madman," shrieked Mrs Arkwright. "That useless criminal Maisie Morris has them."

"No she hasn't. It was me."

All the old people turned and some of them clapped as Mr Cummerbund came forward.

"What?" demanded Mrs Arkwright.

"You heard me," said Mr Cummerbund. "It was me. I stole your hair and teeth. I am sick of you treating Maisie and Mrs Morris badly – they are kind and caring people. And I don't like the way you treat these poor folk either. All they want is to dance and sing and eat nice meals and sometimes go on day trips to Margate, but you lock them up and feed them gruel and they're lucky to see the other end of Withering Heights let alone the Kent coast."

"You?" gasped Mrs Arkwright. "Well, you can jolly well magic me and my poor hus-

band back to our youthful good looks again."

"Ha!" said Mr Cummerbund. "Not likely. Not until you apologize and mend your ways."

Mrs Arkwright was slowly turning a violent shade of purple as she got angrier and angrier.

"Very well, I will find the cure myself. Which room did you say you were in – 3B, isn't it? Come along, Trevor."

Mrs Arkwright swept out of the room and down the stairs, squishing the old people as she went and sending Mr Nidgett spinning down the corridor backwards.

"Follow her!" cried Colonel Snell.

And off they all went to Mr Cummerbund's room.

Mrs Arkwright started frantically throwing things off the shelves. "Gleep remover? What is *gleep*?"

Mr Cummerbund stood patiently beside her. "It's a small parasite made entirely of liver and it attaches itself to your ears and seeps inside. You don't want to know what happens after that."

Maisie nudged him. "Stop her!"

"No," said Mr Cummerbund. "Whatever she does can only do her more harm now. This will be quite interesting."

"Aha!" crowed Mrs Arkwright. "Egyptian age subtracter! This must be the antidote." In her hand was a small brown glass bottle with a squeezy stopper which sucked up a little liquid in a pipette inside.

"I wouldn't if I were you. It's terribly strong!" said Mr Cummerbund. But he was smiling.

"Then I shall take double and make myself look twenty-one again!" said Mrs Arkwright, glaring at him.

"You really should read the instructions, you know," he advised.

But Mrs Arkwright wasn't listening. She undid the stopper and threw it to the ground. Then in one swift movement she opened her puckered-up mouth wide and poured half the bottle down her gullet.

"Yum!" she said, licking her lips. "Like crème de menthe, only with a hint of anchovy." And she prised open Mr Arkwright's mouth and tipped the other half down his throat.

Maisie held her breath. She didn't have long to wait.

"Ouch," said Mrs Arkwright. "I can feel it. It's bubbling and banging in my belly."

"Me too," said Mr Arkwright. "I feel a bit sick."

They looked down at their hands. They were changing. Their fingers

were getting plumper and their liver spots were disappearing.

"Oooh!" chorused the old people.

Then hair started to sprout back through little holes in their scalps.

"Whee!" cried the old people.

Then their wrinkles slowly disappeared and their skin tightened until it was firm and springy. Mr Arkwright's back straightened and Mrs Arkwright's bosom started to grow outwards.

"Steady on, love," said Mr Arkwright.

"How do I look?" asked Mrs Arkwright.

"Radiant!" her husband replied. And she did. Well, as radiant as a nasty selfish person can ever look.

"What about me?"

"You look like a young Mel Gibson," said Mrs Arkwright.

But something wasn't right. They didn't seem to be

stopping. They had started to get shorter.

"What are you doing?" asked Mr Arkwright.

"I'm not doing anything," snapped Mrs Arkwright.

"But look at you."

"Well, look at you too."

They both looked down. They were doing something. They were still going. Mrs Arkwright's big puffy hair had turned itself into an awful seventies flick. She was wearing satin hot pants and platform shoes. Mr Arkwright had long straight hair, a beard and a pair of enormous green flared trousers.

"What's happening?" cried Mrs Arkwright.

"Why am I wearing these awful hippy clothes?" demanded Mr Arkwright.

"You've taken too much," said Mr Cummerbund, hopping with joy. "Oh, this is fascinating! I've never seen this before. Very informative demonstration."

"Well, stop it!" cried Mrs Arkwright.

114

"Oh, I can't," said Mr Cummerbund. "There's no antidote." And he laughed.

"Ggllrmph!" Mrs Arkwright was shrinking again. She now had plaits, knee-length socks and a pleated gym skirt. Mr Arkwright was wearing a cap, short trousers and a rather nasty argyle sweater which looked like his mother had knitted it wearing a blindfold.

"Stop!" said Mr Arkwright. "Stop it at once."

But they weren't stopping. They just carried on getting younger and younger and smaller and smaller until finally...

"Oh my goodness," said Mrs Morris.

"Superb show!" said Colonel Snell.

"Crikey," said Maisie.

On the ground, dressed in nothing but terry towelling nappies and matching bonnets, were Mr and Mrs Arkwright.

"B-b-but ... they're babies," said Maisie, amazed.

"They certainly are," said a deep voice behind them all. "And what bonny things they are as well."

Maisie turned round. In front of her stood the biggest man she had ever seen. His hands were as fat as footballs and he had an enormous black beard.

Maisie gulped. "Boris Kalashnikov," she whispered, and promptly fainted.

Maisie opened her eyes slowly. She felt queasy and was not at all sure what had happened. There were faces in front of her but they were very blurry, as if she were looking at them through a glass with Vaseline on it. She concentrated and tried to focus. Something started swimming into view. It had a beard. Maisie started to sway again.

But someone held her hand.

"It's all right, lovey," said the deep voice. "You're safe now."

Maisie stared hard. It was the same big man from before. "B-b-boris," she stammered.

"Not any more." The giant laughed. "I was for a while, but I got bored of breaking bones."

"He's a florist in Lacking Sidebottom now," said

Mrs Morris, smiling down at her daughter.

"But what about the worms and the rats and the cheese grater?" said Maisie, still shaking.

"I left them in lost luggage at St Pancras, along with my name," answered the man. "You can call me Percy."

Maisie smiled a small weak smile. "What about Mr and Mrs Arkwright?" she asked.

"Well, I don't fancy changing their nappies too much," said Percy. "But plenty of people would give their right kidney for a wee baby. Even if it is Trevor or Cynthia."

"That's right," said Mrs Morris. "Why, with a firm hand and plenty of cod liver oil they might even grow up as nice as you." And she hugged her daughter to her side and smiled. "We'll just have to have them adopted."

Bye-Bye, Baby

And that is exactly what happened. Reg Yonkers, who had turned up with his clipboard and disapproving tone to cart Maisie off to St Strangeway's Home for Horrible Girls, found himself taking a different little girl and boy to a delighted Gladys and Brian Melchett on Acacia Avenue, who called them Imelda and Tarquin.

Mr Cummerbund decided it was time to go as well and called Terry Perry to cart his things to the station.

"I've done all the magic I can here for now. Other folks need my help," he said to Maisie as they stood by the big iron gates of Withering Heights. "Now it's up to you. But I've left you something – look under your bed."

"Bye-bye, Mr Cummerbund," said Maisie sadly.

"Goodbye, Maisie. I'll see you again some day.

And no tears," he said. "Or Groutley will be three feet underwater by tomorrow."

Maisie smiled.

"Bye, Maisie," said Terry Perry, simultaneously cycling and waving with both hands, which was very clever.

"Bye, Terry," said Maisie.

The gates clanked shut and Maisie watched the pair disappear into the distance up Arthur Mallet Road – one hunched old man, brown as a berry with eyes like blackcurrants, and one teenager on a bicycle and cart.

She turned and trudged slowly back to Withering Heights.

"Have a piece of cake, love," said Mrs Morris, trying to stop Jarvis the dog jumping up on her apron.

The pets were all very excited at being let out of the cellar and were causing havoc. Mr Nidgett's parrot was swooping down on the table and stealing Mr Muldoon's liquorice comfits, and several gerbils were nesting in Mr Nidgett's plus fours.

"And stop your awful moping. After tea Colonel Snell is going to teach everyone how to make a sou'wester with a duck and a piece of baling twine, and then we're all going to the Razzmatazz Roller Rink to have popcorn and fizzy gooseberryade."

But Maisie didn't feel much like fizzy pop. "I'm a little tired," she said. "I think I'll lie down for a while."

"You do look a little off colour – I hope you're not going down with that awful gastronomic flu that's going round St Regina's. Bruce Bannister's ma says he's been sick for a week and he's covered in great red spots," said Mrs Morris.

But Maisie was already walking slowly up the stairs.

She sat on her bed, which was playing a soft Russian operatic number, and thought about Mr Cummerbund, the Groutley miracle. She thought about his wonderful suit the colour of an aubergine. She thought about his enormous ears and his eyes like blackcurrants and his kind voice which she would never hear again. A tear rolled down her nose and dripped onto the floor.

Someone – or something – handed her a lemon-scented flannel.

"Thank you," said Maisie and blew her nose.

"Hoop," said the thing.

Maisie wiped her eyes and looked. It was Monkey Onassis. Mr Cummerbund must have forgotten him.

Monkey Onassis had a note in his hairy paws. Maisie prised it off him and opened it. It was written in small joined-up writing.

Dearest Maisie,

I am leaving Monkey Onassis in your care ~ I am sure you will do better than I did at stopping his thieving ways.

Your friend,

Gaston Regis d'Angin Cummerbund

PS Don't let him eat prunes - they do awful things to his digestion.

PSS Don't forget to look under the bed.

Maisie peered under the bed. There was Monkey Onassis's biscuit tin. She pulled it out and lifted the lid.

She gulped. Inside were a pair of sparkly silver tights and dancing shoes. She tried them on. They fitted perfectly.

"You look lovely."

Maisie looked up. It was Loveday Pink.

"Now, come along; we've got work to do if you want to make the Groutley 'Let's Dance' Zinc Medallion competition. Lord knows how I'm going to

teach you the overhead top spin and one-legged honky-tonk in time."

Maisie smiled. And with Loveday Pink on one side and Monkey Onassis on the other, she walked out of the titchy tiny turret and down the spiral stairs.

Epilogue

In case you were worried about what happened after the story ended, I have added this bit just for you.

Mrs Arkwright, or rather Imelda Melchett, was sent to a very strict convent school where she was never allowed to wear make-up or earrings or high heels. She was a plain and serious child who became a nun as soon as she was old enough and was sent to teach religious studies at St Strangeway's Home for Horrible Girls.

Tarquin Melchett, on the other hand, was a precocious show-off who later changed his name and became a rather well-known and flamboyant pop star.

Percy Arkwright never collected his lost luggage. Instead he went back to the florist's in Lacking Sidebottom, where he and his gang of pirates grew gladioli and carnations and won several prizes at the village fête.

Reg Yonkers went back to his mysterious dog droppings on the municipal roses outside the not-so-famous Hosepipe Museum, past the Bernard Gibbons Memorial Multi-Storey Car Park and all the way down to the Razzmatazz Roller Rink.

Mrs Morris took over Withering Heights because she was exactly the right sort of person to run an old people's home – smiley and jolly-faced, who could fix broken pipes and cook squidgy chocolate cake, and who never cheated at Monopoly.

Maisie went on to come second in the Groutley "Let's Dance" Zinc Medallion competition, losing only to the Fawcett Family Dancers, who had the added novelty factor of identical triplets who could walk on their hands while playing kazoos to Ravel's *Boléro*.

Monkey Onassis did not give up his thieving ways but built up a small collection of plastic toys which he stole from cereal boxes in the scullery by emptying all the cereal onto the table.

And Mr Cummerbund?

Well, who knows where he has travelled to? Perhaps he is restoring half boy half yams as I speak. But keep looking out for his purple velvet suit and white hair and quangle stick, because I do believe he may come back one day – maybe even to a town near you.